# THE BEACON

*A Science Fiction Comedy Christmas Play in Two Acts*

## R. J. SULLIVAN

Cover Design by Ash Arceneaux

Page Layout by Bryan Donihue, Section 28 Publishing

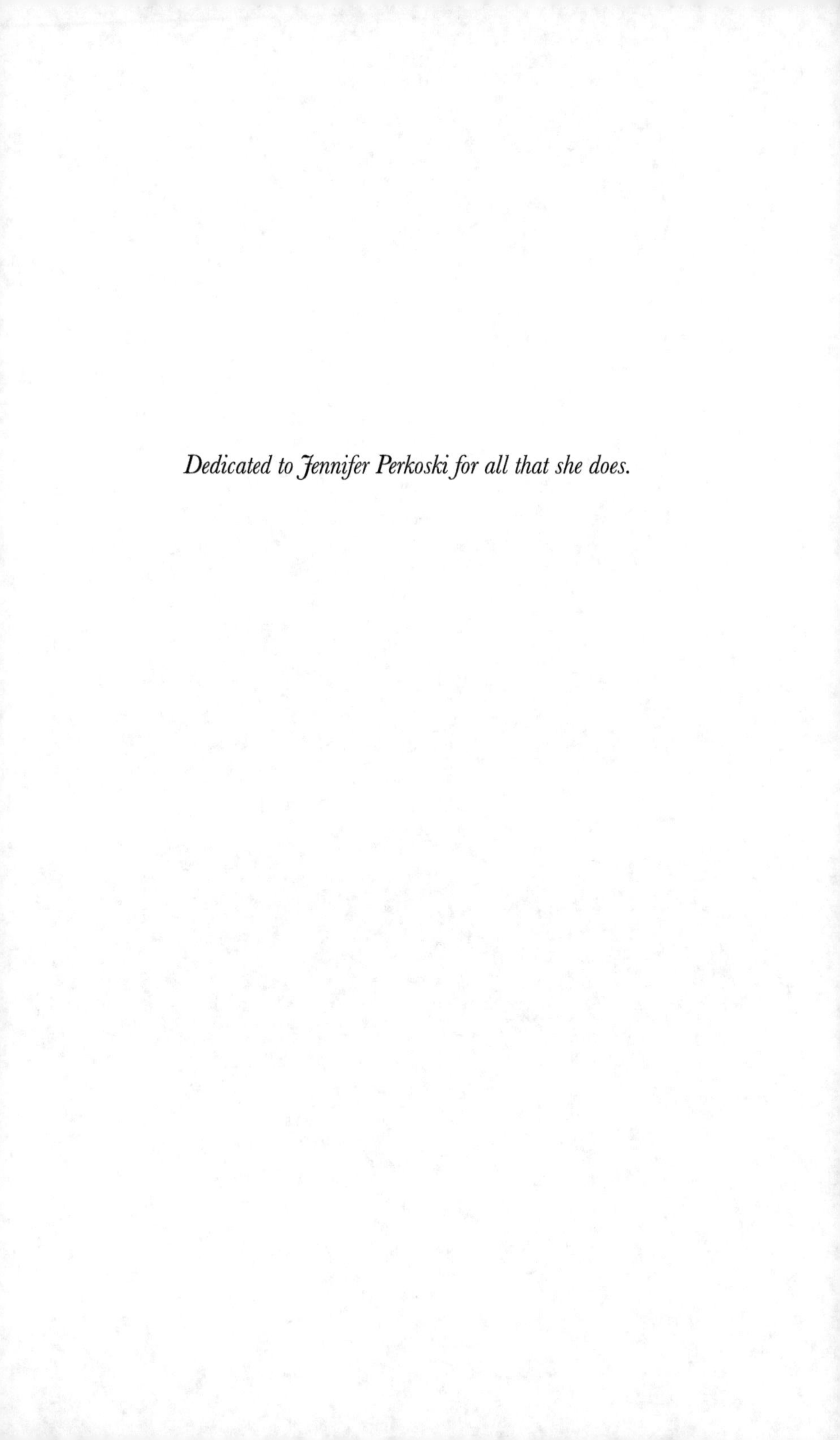

*Dedicated to Jennifer Perkoski for all that she does.*

# NOTES

**Stating what should not have to be stated but this is the world we live in:**

This play is owned by me. Any individual or organization interested in producing the play needs to contact me for permission. I'll make it very easy for you to make that happen, but ask me first. The best first contact to reach me is via my email at *copybob@sbcglobal.net*.

I also welcome fan mail, random hellos, jokes, and other nonsense at the same email address.

# INTRODUCTION

The Beacon was performed before a live audience Saturday, December 16, 2017, at Friendswood Baptist Church in Camby, IN as part of the annual Christmas "Friendswood's Got Talent" show. The cast consisted primarily of our teen group, my son Steven in the role of Graul, my daughters Amanda and Cindy as two wise… persons, and lifelong Trekkie Dena Holmes, who channeled her inner "Shatner" to play Captain Remmer. Dena also provided many of the uniforms and props from her personal Trek collection to help bring it all together.

I can't emphasize enough how fortunate our church is to have Jennifer Perkoski leading our children's music and talent program. The annual talent show has continued to be our most ambitious and challenging year-end program, in which each of us is encouraged to step up and bring our gifts to the stage for His glory.

In January 2017, I approached Jennifer about a science fiction comedy skit and she challenged me to get something on paper to her by June, about five or six pages. Naturally, I turned in over 25 pages in July. Ooops. Well, I thought. I blew that. I guess it won't happen now. Maybe, deep down, I was a bit relieved.

But Jennifer read the skit, got excited about it, and took it to our teen group, who also got excited about it. What followed was a fast track to present a sci-fi spectacle for the stage with sound and video effects, makeup, costumes, and hopefully a whole lot of fun, in under six months for a single performance, not to mention a spare-change budget.

Act 1 was presented at the midway point of the night after several enjoyable music acts and skits. A few more followed, and the night closed with Act II. It all came off without a glitch (as far as anyone in the audience knows) and most people seemed to dig it (A couple of people were certainly not at all sure what to make of what they just saw, but that's okay).

Because we are a small church with limited funds, I purposefully wrote a story with staging as bare-bones as I thought we could get away with. To my surprise, Jennifer, with Dena's help, went way beyond the parameters of the script to create what was, for us, a fairly lavish presentation. The superscripted numbers reference Endnotes at the back of each ACT, and offer further behind-the-scenes anecdotes about how some changes and rewrites became incorporated.

So without any further ado, please enjoy The Beacon.

RJ
August 15, 2018

# SPECIAL THANKS

Special thanks to the cast and crew who participated in the production Saturday, December 16, 2017:

Dena Holmes (Remmer), Eli Bray (Lanson), Steven Sullivan (Graul), Wyatt Perkoski, (Ted), Lily Tranbarger (Angel), Fadol Tiamiou (Shepherd 1), Malik Tiamiou (Shepherd 2)

Nonspeaking parts:
  Mary: Allie Bray
  Joseph: Frankie Perkoski
  Three "Wisepersons": Amanda Sullivan, Cindy Sullivan, Asher Tranbarger
  Shepherds, others: Cassie DeVore, Nevaeh Hayes, Samuel Hess, Micah Hess, Finn Hutchinson, Ryko Hutchinson, Zeke Spencer, Zona Spencer, Farid Tiamiou

Crew: Beth Gilliland, video, sound FX; Whitney Hutchinson: hair and makeup; Amanda Tranbarger: Sound, microphones, videographer.

# CAST

SPEAKING ROLES

## Crew of the USG Starprobe

- **Captain Remmer** - person in space military uniform
- **Pilot Lanson** - person in matching space military uniform
- **Cyborg Mechanic Graul** - person with some robotic, metallic "parts", who also wears variant of space military uniform

NOTE: Crew parts are not boy / girl specific

**Ted the Merciless** - male, flashy space pirate costume, bright garish colors, optional cape, some sort of "power staff" weapon

## Planet-side

- **Angel**
- **Shepherd 1**
- **Shepherd 2**

NONSPEAKING ROLES

**Some shepherd extras**

**Optional "manger scene"**

- **Mary**
- **Joseph**
- **"baby Jesus"**
- **Three Wise Men**

# ACT I

Three chairs in triangular shape, "captain's chair" to the back, front two chairs forward either side of captain's chair. Chairs can have small podiums or desks in front made to look like ship controls.

**REMMER** is in the captain's chair, a side table can be put next to the captain's chair with "controls" where REMMER can hide a tablet.

**LANSON** and **GRAUL** are seated forward. It doesn't matter which side they prefer.

Alternative to podiums or desks, a long table with a "controls console" can be placed in front to seat the front two. A long tablecloth can cover the front.

Tablets with the script can be hidden behind "display panel" props.

A toy laser gun can be put on the table between LANSON and GRAUL, or, alternatively, under Lanson's chair within easy reach.

FBC Note: the back projector can also project the script on it.

# ACT I

On the bridge of the UGC Scoutship *Starprobe*. (see notes)

**REMMER PRE-RECORDED VOICEOVER**
*Ship's Journal number six hundred and five. Captain Remmer recording.*

*The United Galaxy Corps has ordered an emergency relaunch of the UGC Scoutship* Starprobe. *My two crewmembers and I have canceled our scheduled vacation and returned to active duty. We've been ordered to investigate a mystery —a bright star-like object has settled into close orbit around the third planet of the Sol system. The source of this object and the reason for it are both unknown.*

*The third planet is inhabited by a population of nomad tribes and city-kingdoms, centuries away from space travel. Standard UGC protocol applies. We are to investigate, but also make sure that we do not disrupt the natural development of this civilization.*[1]

**[Lights Up, Open Curtains]**[2]

LANSON

Coming up on the third planet, Captain. Faster-than-light drive will cut off in ten seconds.

REMMER

I appreciate the warning, Pilot Lanson. The one time you stopped us without warning, I had to pry my coffee mug from my forehead.

LANSON

[sighs]

You'll never let me forget that, will you?

REMMER

Never.

LANSON

Exiting Faster than Light travel. Settling into orbit around the third planet.

REMMER

Scan the horizon for any visual anomaly.

GRAUL

No need, Captain. It's… pretty obvious.

REMMER

Show me.

**[project "Star of David" in night sky on overhead]**

REMMER

What is it? A new sun?

## LANSON

No, ma'am, scans are jumbled. The readings make no sense.
There's light, but… I can't detect the source. Something beyond this
universe.

## REMMER

It can't just be… a star of light! It's not as if someone can say "let
there be light" and then light just appears. I want answers!

## GRAUL

I've detected something.

## REMMER

An answer?

## GRAUL

Well… no, not an answer, exactly, but another question. According
to our scans, the star is in a geostationary orbit over the planet.

## LANSON

Geo station… *what?*

## GRAUL

The star is positioned directly over a specific land mass above the
planet. It is matching the planet's orbital speed to remain positioned
over that specific land mass.

## REMMER

So… it's *not* a naturally occurring phenomenon, it's… some kind of
beacon. But for what, and why? Lanson, what's directly under
the star?

## LANSON

*[looks at scanner, shakes head]*
Not a lot, even relative to their technology. Seems to be hovering

over a large field near one of their smaller city-dwellings. More
like… Oh… a little town.
*[looks at scanner]*
Of Bethlehem.

REMMER

*[rises and paces]*
Hmmm. How would the sudden appearance of a star like this affect
the people who saw this on the planet?

LANSON

It would probably attract a lot of attention. I imagine travelers
would head toward it in groups to see what's going on.

REMMER

I agree. And that's just what we're going to do as well. Lanson, find
a suitable landing spot for our shuttle. Preferably someplace nearby
but surrounded by trees. We'll land using scanners only, no lights,
and with the engine dampeners on high.

GRAUL

One minute, Captain. I was repairing those systems when we were
called back to duty.

REMMER

You were… what?

GRAUL

The ship needed an overhaul, captain.

REMMER

You were supposed to be on vacation.

GRAUL

As a cyborg, I don't need as much rest as normal humans. The upgrades arrived in spacedock, and, well, the ship wasn't going to fix itself.

REMMER

Fix it *now*, Graul.

GRAUL

Yes, captain, only take a minute to…

**[SFX *red alert blare*]**

LANSON
*[PANICKED]*
SENSORS DETECT A SMALL PIRATE SHIP EXITING FASTER THAN LIGHT! THEIR WEAPONS ARE HOT!

REMMER

Activate defense barrier. Lock on with lasers.

GRAUL

Oh… about that, I was upgrading those when we got called back to active duty.

REMMER

We… don't have defensive barriers?!

GRAUL

Or lasers. But it won't take but a minute….

# [SFX Explosion]

*[all three crew shake around then drop to the floor]*
*[short pause as they lay there]*

### REMMER
*[Sweetly]*
Graul?

### GRAUL
Yes, Captain?

*[Lanson rises and checks the console while Remmer and Graul talk]*

### REMMER
You disconnected the static grip seatbelts, didn't you?

### GRAUL
Yes, but the upgrades will be far superior. We'll never fall out of our
seats again, no matter how large the---

### REMMER
Just… stop… talking.

### GRAUL
Yes, Captain.

### LANSON
*[Excited]*
The pirate ship has docked with us, Captain! Activating the airlock
to board.
*[holds up laser pistol]*
I can stop him!

GRAUL

Actually, the battery is dead.


REMMER

Let me guess. You were going to install upgrades?


GRAUL

No, I… just never hooked it to the recharger.


REMMER

Is there anything on this ship you *didn't* disable?


GRAUL

The bathroom still works.


REMMER

Well, *that's* a relief![3]


*[pause]*


LANSON

You did *not* just say that.


REMMER
*[looking shamefaced]*
I'm afraid I did.


LANSON

Intruder alert, Captain, the invader is just outside the door! Aren't
we going to defend the ship?


REMMER

With what, angry glares?

[Enter Ted the Merciless—flamboyant space pirate costume, with cape, he points some sort of walking stick or rod weapon menacingly][4]


*[Remmer raises hands in surrender, Lanson and Graul follow the captain's example]*

TED

Surrender your ship! You are powerless before the might of... Ted... The Merciless!!

*[pause]*
*[crew tries and fails to stifle laughter]*

LANSON, GRAUL
*[ad lib insults]*
Seriously? Worst name ever. You're joking. Lame. (etc.)

TED
*[stamps foot]*
*Stop it!* You are my prisoners! You will fear me!

REMMER

Did I really just surrender my ship to a space pirate named Ted the Merciless?

LANSON

Why *did* you go with such a terrible name?

TED

It sounded better than Theodore the Merciless.

GRAUL

Well…. he's not wrong about that.

TED
*[stamps foot]*
*Enough!* You will take me to the treasure you've found on the planet and turn it over to me. Do so now and maybe I won't destroy your ship.

REMMER
I thought you just said you were merciless.

TED
Well… I can be a *little* merciful. Sometimes. But only if you do exactly as I say.

LANSON
More like Ted the Clueless.

GRAUL
Ted the Too-Early

*[Graul and Lanson fist bump]*[5]

TED
*[stamps foot, whining]*
*Stop it!* You are my prisoners and will treat me with respect!

REMMER
But they're right. You attacked us too soon. We just got here.

TED
What? You mean you haven't gone down to retrieve the treasure?

REMMER
I'm afraid not.

TED

Then my plan worked *too* well.


LANSON

Yeah. Sure. Go with that.


TED

So here's my *new* brilliant plan. You three will go down and
investigate this *[mispronounces]*
phenomema?


CREW

*[sung to the tune of a popular song sung by puppets]*
♫♫ Do do, do-do-do… ♫♫[6]


TED

Phenomenon?


CREW

♫♫ Do do-do-do… ♫♫


TED

STOP IT!

*[pause]*

You three go down and investigate this… "anomaly", and when you
return with the treasure, I'll take the it from you.


LANSON

Great plan.


GRAUL

You can jump us and catch us by surprise.


*[Lanson and Graul fist bump]*

## REMMER

We were going to investigate anyway. But we have no idea what we'll find. It may not be something we can bring back with us.

## TED

Like what?

## LANSON

If we knew that, we wouldn't have to go down to investigate.

## REMMER

Look, I have a suggestion, Theodore.

## TED

Ted! Ted the Merciless!

## REMMER

Fine… Ted the Merciless. Look, why don't we call a truce for now. You put your weapon away and join our investigation, and then we can get a better idea about what we're dealing with. You have a weapon, and we don't. It's not like we can just gang up on you.

## GRAUL

Actually, that's exactly what we can—

## REMMER

—Shhh!

## TED

Join your investigation. Yes, I like that idea. It's brilliant. I'm glad I thought of it.

## GRAUL

I'm glad he thought of it, too.

LANSON
Ted is merciless *and* wise.
*[Graul and Lanson fist bump]*

TED
I think you are still mocking me, prisoners.

REMMER
Never mind them, Ted. They'll obey my orders.
*[to the crew]*
Graul, Lanson, when Ted puts away his weapon, you will not attack
him. That's a direct order.

GRAUL and LANSON
But captain—

REMMER
—That's a direct order.

GRAUL and LANSON
Yes, captain.

*[Remmer looks at Ted]*

REMMER
One other condition, Ted. I'm in command of the investigation.
You obey *my* orders.

TED
What? Absolutely not!

REMMER
Then you can investigate the phenomenon by yourself.

TED

*[begrudgingly]*
Fine. You're in command.


REMMER

Great. Now put away your weapon.


TED

Okay, but no tricks! Ted the Merciless is not easily fooled!


LANSON

Oh, we *know* that.


GRAUL

Ted the Merciless is *impossible* to fool.


*[Lanson and Graul fist bump]*


TED

*[whining]*
They're still mocking me!


REMMER

Lanson, set us down, somewhere in the woods. Turn off the exterior
lights and use the engine dampeners. Unless you….
*[glares at Graul]*


GRAUL

The engine dampeners are fully functional, Captain.


REMMER

Whew, that's good. Graul, program the costume replicator to fit us
with clothing that will help us blend in.


TED

Order them to stop mocking me!

**REMMER**
You really are a baby, Theodore.


**LANSON**
Landing spot detected, Captain. Preparing to land the ship.


**[SFX: Ship descending]**


**[Lights Out - END OF ACT I]**

---

1. In the FBC production, the audio opened with a piece of free audio space adventure music while the screen overhead had a "warp effect" visual. The journal entry was pre-recorded and added to the video. The lights then came up on Lanson's first line.
2. The command center had a detailed "classic Star Trek"-inspired backdrop. Remmer had a raised "captain's chair" and Lanson and Graul were positioned lower, both seated behind a long table. "Keep it simple," she said. "We don't have much money," she said....
3. An audio FX "rimshot" sounded here to make sure no one missed the poop joke.
4. It was, in fact, a groovy light-up pirate sword.
5. The actors ad-libbed a recurring joke where Graul couldn't fist bump properly.
6. This is an homage the old "Muppet Show Mah Na Man Na" skit" (you can actually find it on YouTube under that name). The gag happened organically during rehearsals.

# ACT II

# SETTING FOR ACT II
## BETHLEHEM / OPTIONAL MANGER

Open fields in Bethlehem; optional manger scene Stage Right

Stage is cleared, maybe some props to indicate a field.

Extreme stage right a group of shepherds

Extreme Stage Left can be an optional abridged manger scene:
Mother Mary, Joseph, baby Jesus, three wise men, some animals.

Alternatively, crew can go off Stage Left when manger interactions
are described.

# ACT II

An open field in Bethlehem. See notes.

**[Lights Up, Open Curtains]**

*[REMMER, LANSON, GRAUL and TED enter from off stage wearing shepherd cloaks]*

*[Optional visual gags: TED still has his garish space pirate costume on with a shepherd cloak or maybe just the hat. GRAUL has mechanical parts clearly visible. Maybe someone is dressed as a sheep.]*[1]

**[Star of David on overhead projection]**

REMMER

Everyone remember where we parked!

LANSON

On it, captain!

# [SFX: Key Alarm]

GRAUL
*[turns toward overhead, shields eyes]*
We're practically under the beacon. Whatever's going on, it can't
be far.

TED
Maybe we need to start digging! Aren't all valuable treasures
buried?

LANSON
Sure, why don't you get started on that?

REMMER
Lanson, don't be rude.

LANSON
*[contrite]*
Yes, Captain.

REMMER
Do you see any unusual activity on the scanners?

LANSON
*[holds out tablet, speaks directly out to audience]*
You mean these high tech flat screen scanning devices we're all
carrying with us that absolutely are *not* tablets with our lines
on them?

REMMER
*[conspicuously looking at tablet]*
Why, yes, Lanson, those devices.[2]

## LANSON
One moment.
*[pause]*
Yes, there's a strange energy signature in this direction.
*[points Stage Right to where shepherds are clustered]*

## REMMER
Okay, let's go investigate. But remember, blend in!

*[REMMER, LANSON, GRAUL, and TED go down the steps in the direction of the shepherd group]*

*[ANGEL enters stage right, shepherds cower and fall to their knees. Ship crew stops advancing and stares, stunned]*

## ANGEL
Do not be afraid. I bring you good news that will cause great joy for all the people. Today in the town of David a Savior has been born to you; he is the Messiah, the Lord. This will be a sign to you: You will find a baby wrapped in cloths and lying in a manger.

## SHEPHERDS and ANGEL
Glory to God in the highest heaven,
and on Earth, peace to those on whom his favor rests.

*[ANGEL EXITS]*

## SHEPHERD 1
Perhaps the angel means Mary and Joseph, two travelers from Nazareth. I spoke to the inn keeper earlier tonight. She settled Mary and Joseph in the barn, because there were no rooms left.

## SHEPHERD 2
We should go to Bethlehem and see for ourselves if what the angel has told us is true.

*[shepherd group walks past the ship crew, who stand, wave, smile, trying and failing to blend in. Shepherds ignore them and enter the stable]*

### REMMER
*[to Lanson]*
Tell me you scanned all that.

### LANSON
Well… yes, but the readings make no sense. The messenger… being… seems made of light similar to the star overhead.

### GRAUL
The shepherds called it an angel.

### REMMER
"Angel?" I have no idea what that is.

### GRAUL
If the beacon above us is controlled by some entity of great power, this angel may be a servant to that entity.

### REMMER
Curious. The mystery deepens.

### TED
And we still don't know what the treasure is. What is a…messiah? And how much can I get for it on the black market?[3]

### GRAUL
According to my data banks, the term Messiah refers to a great ruler that liberates their people.

### REMMER
What did the angel say? "You will find the baby wrapped in cloths and lying in a manger"

TED
What's a manger? And how much can I get for it on the black market?

GRAUL
A manger is a food trough for animals, usually within a barn.

TED
Gross!

LANSON
So this "awesome leader" was just born… in a barn? That doesn't sound very awesome to me.

GRAUL
A person's greatness is not necessarily determined by one's birth.

REMMER
[dramatically]
A child born in a barn, yet… the night sky itself proclaims his arrival!
[pause]
We need to go see this great leader for ourselves.

GRAUL
[consulting tablet, points Stage Left]
Easy to find, Captain. Several life forms have been closing in on the wooden structure directly under the star in this direction.

[Wise men walk up and enter the stable]

LANSON
So… there it is.

[All turn toward the stable]

GRAUL

Three visitors have just entered the barn. They… appear to be
ambassadors of some importance.

REMMER

Scan all of this and get a video record, Graul.

GRAUL

Yes, captain.
*[points device]*

**[Video of stable scene is projected on overhead screen]**

GRAUL

The ambassadors appear to be offering treasures, presumably of
some value.

TED

Treasures? What sort of value?

GRAUL

Scanning. They appear to be… gifts of gold, frankincense
and myrrh.

TED

Gold! Yes! Gold is worth a lot on the black market!

TED

And, Uh…. what were those other two?

GRAUL

My database says Frankincense is incense from France.

TED

Well, it sounds pretty obvious when you put it that way.

GRAUL

Frankincense and myrrh have a pleasant aroma when burned, myrrh can be used as a perfume, both have medicinal qualities as a disinfectant.

TED

Perfume and incense? Not as awesome as gold, but I'll take it!

*[TED steps toward the manger]*

*[REMMER grabs him by the shoulder and holds him back]*

REMMER

The beacon isn't here to tell people about gold or perfume. It's about pointing people to the birth of a great leader.

TED

You're right! We'll steal the baby.[4]

REMMER

*[appalled]*
We are not stealing the baby!

TED

Fine. You're so smart, *you* tell *me* what we're going to steal.

REMMER

How about you and I just go inside and see what's going on.

TED

Gather more intel! Brilliant idea. Glad I thought of it.

REMMER

*[Points to LANSON and GRAUL]*
You two stay back in case we run into trouble.

*[REMMER and TED walk into stable.]*

*[While GRAUL speaks, LANSON is looking around as if watching for any potential danger outside.]*

GRAUL
*[looking at his scanner]*[5]
They're going into the barn. Everyone in the barn has turned to look at Ted.

LANSON
What's Ted doing?

GRAUL
He's looking silly.

LANSON
Sounds about right.

GRAUL
Remmer is pushing him forward. They're both going up. The mother, Mary…. wow, she's… she's radiant.

LANSON
I hear new mothers get that way.

GRAUL
No, this is something different. Oh. Looks like Ted wants to hold the baby but Joseph isn't very happy.

LANSON
Can't blame him for that.

GRAUL
Mary is saying it's okay. Ted's got the baby. Wow.

LANSON
What's up?

GRAUL
I don't know. Ted looks… different.

LANSON
Less silly?

GRAUL
Well, no, but… less like a jerk, I guess. Almost like a decent person.

LANSON
Sounds like you need to adjust the focus.

GRAUL
The captain is nudging Ted. Ted won't give up the baby.
*[pause]*
Uh-oh.

LANSON
We're gonna have to make a run for it, aren't we?

GRAUL
Joseph has stepped forward. No, it's okay, Ted passed the baby to
Remmer. Hey, how long have you known the captain?

LANSON
About five years, why?

GRAUL
That's about how long I've known (him/her), too. But I've never
seen (him/her) look like this. Check it out.

*[LANSON takes GRAUL's scanner and looks into the screen.]*

LANSON

*[Genuine, no snark]*
Wow. The captain looks both overjoyed and overwhelmed. (He/she) didn't look that happy and stunned when they promoted (him/her) to captain three years ago. Uh-oh. Now it looks like the captain doesn't want to give up the baby.

GRAUL

Should we try to get them out of there or just make a run for the ship?

LANSON

No, false alarm. Remmer's handed the baby back to Mary.

GRAUL

Now if they would just get out of there—

LANSON

Hold it. They—that is, the Captain and Ted—both just dropped to their knees with the rest of the group.

GRAUL

They did? Why?

LANSON

I have no idea. Okay, they're getting up.

**[Overhead fades out, replaced by original image]**

*[REMMER and TED rejoin LANSON and GRAUL Center stage. REMMER and TED look dazed and amazed, having just been in the presence of Jesus]*

LANSON

Captain, are you okay?

GRAUL

Do you require medical attention?


REMMER

[waving them off]

I don't think so, I just need a minute.


TED

I also just need some time to recover.


GRAUL

We didn't ask.


LANSON

We don't care.


GRAUL

[to Remmer]

Is there anything we can get you?


LANSON

Perhaps if we overpower Ted and throw him in our holding cell, the captain will recover faster.


TED

I'm standing right here!


REMMER

[recovering]

No… Ted's no longer a threat to us. He's no longer a threat to anyone. I suspect he doesn't want to be known as Ted the Merciless anymore.

[directly to TED]

Isn't that right?

TED

No, I… that is, I've decided it's time for a career change. My mother
was always disappointed that I never finished medical school.

LANSON

Wait… you want to become, what, Doctor Ted, Medicine Pirate?

TED

Doctor Ted, Medicine Pirate! That's great! I'm glad I
*[pause]*
… I mean, I'm glad *you*… thought of it.[6]

LANSON
*[to GRAUL]*
You're the brilliant one, what's going on?

GRAUL

I am at as much of a loss to explain what has happened as you are.

REMMER
*[dramatically]*
It was… that baby. Once I looked into the face of the baby,
everything made sense. The star, the angel, suddenly, the universe all
made sense.

LANSON

Captain, you're babbling.

REMMER
*[dramatic, rambling]*
I know, but… don't you see? Graul, put aside your doubt and hear
me out. Imagine, a stupendous being… beyond our comprehension,
beyond science, beyond the supernatural. Imagine a being that has
taken guardianship of this planet and the people that live here.
Maybe even created it. Now it wants to change their lives. It wants

them to be… greater… than they are. It's worked with them, guided them, often he's been angry with them, but also infinitely patient. Now… he's giving them a gift. A… savior!

GRAUL

Captain, what you are describing is a blatant violation of the noninterference—

REMMER

—I'm talking about an entity that exists beyond to our rules, laws and restrictions.
*[GRAUL and LANSON exchange worried looks]*

LANSON

Captain, that's… extraordinary.

TED

That's right. Your captain is exactly right. I felt it, too.

GRAUL

Felt what, exactly?

TED

The star above us. The beacon. Think of it as the universe's largest birthday candle.

LANSON
*[exasperated]*
Ted, will you please stop talking?

REMMER
But… Ted is right.

LANSON and GRAUL
Whaaat?

## REMMER

The star. It's a beacon to tell the world, "tonight, your savior, my son, has been born. Follow the star to greet him and to celebrate his birth."

## LANSON

But captain… he's just a child. Who is he here to save?

## REMMER

He's here to save everyone. He's here to save this planet.

## GRAUL

Save them from what?

## REMMER

The people on this planet are just like all the beings we've met in our explorations. They're just like us, for that matter. They can be good, but too much of the time, they choose not to be. Someday, and I have no idea how, this child is going to save the people of this planet… from themselves.

## GRAUL

Captain, listen to yourself. Even if what you say is true, how can this savior get a message out to everyone on this planet? These people travel on the backs of animals and they communicate with paper scrolls. For a savior to get a message out to the entire world, it would take… a miracle!

## REMMER

Yes, Graul, it will take a miracle. A miracle like a gigantic glowing star of light without matter.

## GRAUL

Captain, if you're right, and this king has come to save this planet, how do you account for the beacon attracting our ship as well?

REMMER

I'm still not sure about that. I'd like to think our being here isn't just a random event, that it will serve some kind of greater good, but I just don't know what that might be… yet.


TED

*[to himself looking at his tablet]*
I wonder how much a medical kit will cost on the black market?


LANSON

*[motions toward Ted]*
I don't know Captain, a space pirate re-dedicating his life to helping others might qualify as accomplishing a greater good.


TED

*[looks up]*
What?


REMMER

Never mind. Come on, Ted, let's get you back to your ship.


*[RIMMER and TED slowly head up the steps]*


GRAUL

Captain. If this entity that you describe truly created this planet, and then sent a great king that can save everyone on it, it's possible that this entity also created the entire universe.


REMMER

Yes, anything's possible. There are many mysteries throughout the cosmos that we haven't yet solved, my friend.

GRAUL

It's interesting to consider. The entity that sent a great king to save this world could send a savior to other worlds. He could send a savior to all of them. Perhaps one day we'll see a similar miracle on our own world. Perhaps, as we continue to explore other worlds, we'll see more signs of His majesty all throughout the cosmos.

## REMMER

Perhaps we will, now that we know what to look for. But not tonight. Personally, I'm good with this one life-altering miracle for one day. Come on, crew, let's go home.

**[End of Act II]**

---

1. They went pretty silly, of course. Remmer dressed as a shepherd, Lanson a sheep, and Graul looked like a big golden "Hardee's" star.
2. I knew I was asking a lot of three main characters, so I figured having the tablets would help, and why not make it a gag since they were carrying them anyway.
3. An SFX of "cha-ching" cash register followed each uttering of "black market".
4. I still can't believe they left this joke in.
5. Rather than act out the manger scene to the side or let the descriptions stand, our production projected a video of the manger scene that was filmed earlier in the week that plays out as described while Lanson and Graul synched their dialog to the pre-recorded image. Another case of going the extra mile.
6. This external demonstration of Ted's change of heart was exactly what was needed at the right place in the story. As much as I wish I could say that I thought of it myself (like Ted does), it's a line change added by Jennifer as rehearsals were underway. Brilliant.

# ABOUT THE AUTHOR

*The Beacon is a standalone science fiction play, but if you enjoyed this, you might also enjoy R.J.'s spaceship science fiction adventure novel* Commanding the Red Lotus *or his short story collection of science fiction and fantasy* Darkness with a Chance of Whimsy, *both published through Seventh Star Press. R.J.'s short fiction has appeared in the acclaimed anthologies* Vampires Don't Sparkle *and* Dark Faith: Invocations. *Learn more at* http://www.rjsullivanfiction.com

facebook.com/R.J.SullivanAuthor

twitter.com/rjsullivanauthr

# BLUE CHRISTMAS

*A Rebecca Burton and Blue Shaefer Holiday Story*

R. J. SULLIVAN

Cover Design by Nell Williams

Page Layout by Bryan Donihue, Section 28 Publishing

*Dedicated to Beverly Bullock*
*April 4, 1965-December 23, 2013*
*Our Christmas Angel*

# Notes

"Blue Christmas" originally appeared in the anthology *Gifts of the Magi*, a holiday collection co-edited by John F. Allen, E. Chris Garrison, and R.J. Sullivan

Author's note: *Ahoy, thar be spoilers ahead!* "Blue Christmas" takes place after *Haunting Blue* and *Virtual Blue*.

# Blue Christmas

A REBECCA BURTON AND BLUE SHAEFER HOLIDAY
STORY

Fiona "Blue" Shaefer sat in the living room of her boyfriend's father's home on Christmas Eve in somber reflection. She sipped a Sprite and cuddled with Chip on the couch. The artificial but lovely tree with its blinking lights filled the space with holiday ambiance. While it was nice, it was also pretty weird.

Behind them, through swinging western doors, "The Two Dads", James Farren and Paul Willis, sat at the breakfast nook, warming up to each other as they took down a six pack of bottled beer. Normally, the proximity of "The Two Dads" would have dampened the romance, but overall, given the excitement of the past two years, this was pretty peaceful. Almost…dare she think it… *domestic*.

Not a word Blue tended to apply to herself.

Here she was, back in the small bumpkin town of Perionne, Indiana, contrary to all her plans to leave this town and *never, ever* come back. But this was a chance to spend a peaceful, quiet Christmas with her boyfriend, and after all they'd been through, she was okay with that. *Though it's definitely weird.*

The doorbell rang, and Blue offered Chip a questioning look.

He held up his phone. "Go ahead, I'm finishing a text."

"Nerd," she said, but she flashed him a smile as she stood.

Blue recognized the tall, distinguished figure standing under the porch light. Rebecca Burton, Special Investigations Unit Agent and infuriating pain in Blue's ass the previous month, wore her distinctive black fedora, matching leather jacket, business casual blouse and blue jeans. In one arm, she cradled a wine bottle.

Long, bright red hair curtained Burton's serious expression. She extended the bottle. "Peace offering? Merry Christmas."

Blue had no idea what stupid stunned expression she returned. Only one thought spun through her head. *Oh, crap, tonight just got a whole lot weirder.*

Burton waited out Blue's moment of shock with her characteristic stoic expression.

The moment passed, and Blue gave in to a petulant streak. "What makes you think I'm at all interested in a peace offering from you?"

Burton consulted the label. She pinched one side of her glasses with two fingers as she read, "Sweet Inspiration, red port dessert wine, rich raspberry and chocolate flavor, bottled locally by Cedar Cr—"

"Please come in." Blue stepped to the side to make room for Burton to step past.

Chip looked up from his phone. A sharp intake of breath revealed his surprise, but he recovered fast. "Rebecca, it's... good to see you."

"And you, Eugene."

"The Two Dads" had already stepped into the room, now a wall of parental concern. Shoulder to shoulder, they crossed their arms and made clear their demand that someone damn well better explain themselves.

Blue went first. "Dad, uh... Mr. Farren, this is Rebecca Burton.

Chip and I... hung out with her... at Indiana University... over Thanksgiving Break," she finished lamely.

Rebecca Burton, in fact, was a government agent who had saved Chip and Blue from certain death during their wild encounter with a cultist group that had taken over Chip's video game and sent them all on the wildest and most dangerous encounter of their lives—and that was saying something.

In the weeks since, for several practical reasons, Chip and Blue hadn't hinted a word about this encounter to either of their fathers.

Paul gave voice to the obvious. "Ms. Burton seems a bit old to be a full-time student."

"Oh, I'm not a student," said Burton, who reached into her coat and produced her badge. "Rebecca Burton, Special Investigations Unit. I was... on site offering my services to assist the local police on an urgent matter over the holidays. Chip was an invaluable asset."

James Farren, a computer engineer himself, scrutinized her credentials. "How did two college students help with a state investigation?"

Rebecca's answered without hesitation. "The university was trying to deal with some pretty sophisticated computer hackers. Eugene came highly recommended, and in fact, they both assisted me that weekend. Thanks to them, we broke up a ring of cyberterrorists."

Blue averted her eyes. *Damn, smooth as butter. If I didn't know she was lying her ass off, I'd have no idea.* She felt her father's stare upon her and knew her face flared pink. Even in the room of colorful blinking lights, she wondered if he noticed.

Mr. Farren handed Rebecca her badge. "Sounds exciting."

"In fact, I'm here to discuss using their services again. I'd pay them, of course."

Mr. Farren stayed on topic. "Chip never said a word about you, Ms. Burton."

"Neither did Fiona," added Paul.

"Well, it wasn't really a big deal," Chip began.

"You assisted with a criminal conspiracy and didn't see it worth mentioning?"

Blue started, "I'm sorry, Dad, it was a crazy weekend—"

Rebecca stepped forward. "What Fiona means is, they were sworn to secrecy while we worked out the legalities of the case." She placed a hand on each father's forearm. From where she stood, Blue saw her father's eyes widen. Blue knew that, with skin to skin contact, Rebecca could channel considerable powers of psychic persuasion.

"You are both concerned, and, believe me, I understand. We are leaving now, but your children will be safe under my care. Please don't let this ruin your evening. I'll bring them home in a couple of hours."

In the silence that followed, Blue's pulse throbbed against her temples.

Mr. Farren looked at her dad. "That's fine with me. Want another beer, Paul?"

"I think I'm due. Have fun, you guys."

As "The Two Dads" retreated into the kitchen, Burton turned her back and addressed Chip and Blue. "Let's go. I'll fill you in on the way."

"You promised us wine," said Blue.

"Later."

"Wait a minute," said Blue. "What makes you think we're going with you? And... my God, Rebecca, do you need a carry permit for those hands?"

"Your mother is in danger."

That stung. "My mother is dead!" A flood of guilt froze her in mid-step. For the past few years, the specter of her mother could only visit her, briefly, in dreams and visions. And while Blue cherished those moments, it didn't make her mother any less murdered.

Rebecca glanced back at the two parents, who looked oblivious to their exchange, before she hissed. "Her spiritual presence in this realm is in danger. If we don't act, she may be cut off from this world. Forever."

"Lead the way," said Chip as he pulled the door shut behind them.

They strode through the lovely night of fallen snow and dancing flurries, a perfect Indiana "White Christmas" Eve. *This would have been a nice night to walk with Chip through the neighborhood while we kept each other warm with Christmas wishes.*

*So much for that plan.*

Blue followed Rebecca to a sky-blue Buick. The last time Blue had seen it, the car had a shattered window, now replaced. Blue and Chip opened the back doors and got in, for no other reason than that they'd ridden in the back seat last time, when Rebecca's assistant Skye MacLeod had ridden shotgun.

*And if I'm totally honest, Rebecca still creeps me out.* Aloud, she asked, "Where are we going?"

"Your house."

"My...?" *Oh.* Technically, Blue had inherited her mother's property in Perionne, the home where her mother had been murdered in cold blood. A house Blue vowed never set foot in again. A house perpetually for sale in the years since. Though the property promised future money if the sale ever happened, the real estate agent faced one problem, a nearly insurmountable one. As far as the town was concerned, the property was one of two haunted houses in Perionne—houses right next to each other.

Sylvia Stalt, the mother of the most notorious criminal in Perionne, had lived and died in one. And the home next door was the site of her mother's grisly murder.

Most people had no idea of another connection between the homes—that the notorious criminal, temporarily awakened in spirit form—had committed the grisly murder. The killing had rendered Blue parent-less, at least until word reached her estranged father in New York.

Blue realized that Rebecca followed the short route from Chip's house to her mother's. She swallowed back bile. "I... really don't want to go there."

"We have no choice," said Rebecca. "A cult of ghost-hunting

druids has already gathered at your home. They're going to attempt to contact and exorcise the spirits residing there."

"Who tipped you off?" asked Blue.

"The Transit King. He's an informant from the fairy world who travels the public roadways. He frequently comes upon information of a paranormal nature."

"So what's it to him?"

"I suspect he knew this lead would put me in his debt."

"Okay, then." Had anyone else said this, Blue would think they were bonkers, but she knew better than to scoff.

Rebecca continued. "If they succeed, they could banish your mother from the physical realm. Permanently."

"Is that likely?" Normally, Blue approved of vanquishing ghosts, but not when that ghost was her mom.

"I trust you are familiar with *A Christmas Carol* by Charles Dickens."

"Of course."

"Dickens set that story on Christmas Eve for a reason. It's a night when people all over the world remember loved ones no longer with them, and that makes it easier for some specters to interact with the living, if only for a few seconds."

Blue couldn't deny that memories of past Christmases with her mom had already broken in on her holiday. As much as they'd fought through the years, they'd always called a truce during Christmas.

In the dark, Chip's hand found Blue's, first tentatively, then enfolding hers in a clasp. Blue psyched herself. *Whatever comes next, I'll be damned if anyone's going to take what's left of my mother away from me.*

❧

Doug Faddon shifted his bulk on the living room couch of the late Leona Shaefer. The house, infamous after the murder committed within its walls two years ago, had no working electricity; the candles his two companions had smuggled in failed to reach the

edges of the room where the shadows dwelled. *What am I doing here? Why am I breaking and entering on Christmas Eve to hold this stupid séance instead of sitting at home with my parents eating Christmas Eve dinner?*

Liz Dooley, seated on the other side of the couch, flashed a bashful grin his direction, her wavy blond hair radiant in the candlelight.

*Oh, who am I kidding? I know* exactly *why I'm here.*

Sheets and cloths covered each piece of furniture to protect it from dust and decay, coverings which, ironically, now yellowed and were caked in dust from years of dormancy. The telltale squeaks under his ass told him he sat on leather — soft, cushy, expensive leather.

Last week in Chemistry, Liz had asked him to join her on this adventure. Flattered to be asked, he agreed without hesitation.

Liz had explained, "Claire said we need a third person, and Karen is going to be out of town. Claire was pretty miffed when she heard, too, because Karen has the strongest aura of all three of us," Liz said, as if that made perfect sense.

Doug knew Claire Grattick from Algebra. She was a brainy girl, but also kinda' bossy, always in the back of the classroom with other girls gathered 'round. She whispered in harsh tones while they giggled and pointed and called each other "sisters" even though there was no way they came from the same family. "What is it, anyway, a school club?"

"Sorta," said Liz. "Kinda new age. We get together and memorize spells and use crystals and stuff."

He had no idea what she meant, but he suspected Pastor Jeff would not approve. Still, when she fixed him with her icy blue eyes, he didn't care, either.

"We're going to the Shaefer house to see if we can talk to the dead mom."

"No way." He knew all about Fiona Shaefer and her dead mother. Doug was a Freshman in 2010 when all that craziness had hit.

"Way." Liz grinned, causing Doug to swoon. "So, are you in? She said I could pick anyone I wanted."

He'd agreed, but then when he showed up this evening, they'd both found out that Liz had misunderstood an important detail.

"A... *boy*?" Claire had erupted as soon as Doug approached the house. "You asked a *boy* to join *our* circle?"

Crestfallen, Doug hung back several paces.

Liz pouted. "You said I could bring *anyone,* as long as I had a strong connection with them!"

Claire fumed. "I meant...oh, never mind."

*Liz has a strong connection with me?* Doug's heart beat faster at her words.

Liz and Doug had been friends for months. She shared all sorts of things with him—favorite movies, favorite songs, teachers she wanted to punch in the face — nothing he thought of as deep. For his part, he'd sit, and nod, and fantasize, too scared to speak his feelings aloud. Liz always finished, "You're such a terrific listener, I can tell you anything."

Liz tried to explain, but Claire just made a noise of disgust and turned her back.

"Look," said Doug. "I don't need this. My parents are worried, anyway, and—"

"No," muttered Claire, "we need three for the spell. Better a man than no one."

"Thanks for nothin'."

Behind Claire's back, Liz flashed him a radiant smile, rolled her eyes, and extended her hand. "She just doesn't know you like I do."

That was an hour ago, and Claire had hardly said a word since. Instead, she'd wandered around the front room while she rattled some rocks, lined up candles around the edge of the room, and waved her hands in the air while muttering to herself. In the meantime, Liz flashed him coy looks, only to turn away whenever he tried to meet her gaze.

For his part, Doug tried to enjoy being in the company of two women, while also trying to ignore the potent aroma of incense and

being down the hall from the scene of one of the worst crimes in Perionne history.

Claire lit the final candle, a large red votive one that set in a base holder in the middle of the room. They'd moved the coffee table aside some time ago, and now Claire sat, cross-legged in the middle of the floor before the candle. The flame lit the bottom half of her face to give her what Doug thought of as "super villain lighting," though he didn't dare say so out loud.

Claire motioned for Doug and Liz to join her. "Gather around."

Liz dropped down smoothly, but for Doug, the trip to the floor proved more of a challenge. He stifled a wince, not wanting to draw attention to his general problem of being terribly out of shape.

Now seated in a rough triangle around the candle, Claire extended a hand to each of them.

Liz placed her hand in Claire's and extended her other hand to him.

*God, I hope my palms aren't sweaty.* Doug wiped his hands across the legs of his jeans. Hoping he looked casual, he reached to either side and closed the circle.

Claire returned a firm grip, while Liz's hand, he couldn't help but notice, trembled.

"Brace yourselves," Claire said. "We're gathered in a place of unique convergence on a night of great spiritual activity. We sit in proximity to, not just one gateway to the spirit realm, but two."

"Two?"

Liz tipped her head toward the house next door. "This house, and Sylvia's home next door."

Doug heard himself gulp. "Spirits from the *Stalt* house may join us?"

"Anything is possible." Clare's hand squeezed Doug's in sudden urgency. "This is why we must focus on our true intentions tonight. We're here to contact Leona Shaefer, to get to the truth of her murder, and perhaps learn the identity of her murderer."

*We are?* Doug considered. *Why go through all this to contact a spirit just to make her recount the most traumatic moment of her life? We already*

9

*know she was awakened by an intruder, tried to defend herself, and was killed anyway.*

"Leona," Claire called, "hear our voice. Come to us. Tell us your story, so you can be at peace, leave this house, and cross into the spiritual realm." After a pause, "We're here to help you."

To Doug's shock, a voice answered. A dry, crackling voice, like dried leaves. "Now, that's a lie, and you know it, girlie. You've no interest in helping her, none whatsoever."

Startled, Doug turned to the source of the voice.

In the corner, in the recliner, sat Sylvia Stalt. Still rocking, and her hands still knit on the shapeless whatever-it-was over her lap.

The sight brought back memories, mostly unpleasant, of his childhood encounters with Sylvia while she still lived. The creepy old lady spent years freaking out every kid who drifted anywhere near her porch, sharing bizarre stories and, in retrospect, words of wisdom. She'd warned him more than once to "stop guzzlin' all that-thar' soda and snarfin' all them-thar' candy bars or you'll surely catch the 'Bee-dees'." He'd always run home to his mother, who promptly gave him another soda to calm his nerves.

Last year, the family doctor had put him on oral insulin.

Still, he'd greeted the news of her death with relief. The last thing he wanted was to see her here in the living room.

"Go on, girlie," Sylvia taunted, "tell the truth for once in yer life. Or I suppose I should say...yer pathetic existence."

The front door rattled.

Doug jumped, alarmed. If he could have coordinated his limbs, he would have stood and run for it, but he was on the ground, stuck. *Oh, my God, who's that? Who's that? There's a ghost at the door, there's...*

Liz looked from the door to Claire, to Doug, and back again, her eyes wide.

*Oh my God, the door's still rattling! We need to*—and with that, the door burst open...and a figure stepped through. In the dim light, Doug could barely make out a female form.

As the figure came forward, Doug's heart skipped. *Leona! It's her!*

*She's back from the grave to*—Then he noticed the blue tint to the woman's hair, and recognition set in. *Fiona? It's Fiona.*

Fiona wasted no time with pleasantries. "Get the hell out of my house! All of you."

Liz spoke first. "*Your* house? But I thought the owner was dead."

"Wrong." Fiona held up a ring of keys. One key hung limply. "The house was left to me, and that makes you all trespassers."

Doug released Liz's hand. "We're sorry, we didn't mean it."

Liz looked ready to tear up.

Claire, however, refused to release his hand. "Ignore her, don't break the circle."

Liz's eyes flashed anger. "Y'know, this was fun, but I'm done now."

"No kidding," said Doug.

"Don't you dare, not until my revenge is complete."

"Revenge?" Blue exclaimed, matching Doug's internal thought exactly. "Get out, or there's going to be trouble."

"Not until I've reached your mother."

Sylvia spoke up. "Not gonna happen, girlie. I already warned Leona away. She's under my protection."

Claire snarled. "Fine. Then I'll go through you to get to her."

"Wait," shouted Blue. "Who are you? What do you want with my mother?"

A tall, authoritative presence entered behind Fiona. "Be cautious, Fiona. She's not who she appears to be."

Claire cackled, and Doug did a double take at the noise.

"What's the matter, don't recognize me? Or rather, who I used to be?"

"Get out of the house or I'll throw you out."

As Claire rose to her feet, she drew out a knife, though Doug missed where it had come from.

"Remember, Blue? I told you the last time we met that I'd find a way back. And when I did, I'd find a way to destroy everyone you love."

Fiona's eyes widened. "Marda!"

Doug watched, baffled. He was done with the prank. He just wanted to go home.

Though the body before her stood taller and had a more athletic build, Blue recognized the insane expression on the face, the same as the woman Blue had killed two months ago... *in self defense, it was self defense.*

The Marda stand-in motioned with her knife. "Clear the way to the door, and I'll let you all live."

Blue scoffed. "If you're really Marda, you couldn't successfully stab a *piñata* if you were straddling it with both knees."

Instead of moving toward the door, the Marda stand-in dropped to her knees behind the timid blond and brought her blade to the girl's throat.

Blue didn't take her eyes off the blade. She recognized the design, the ceremonial knife used by the Sisterhood of Baalina, identical to the one she'd taken from the flesh-and-blood Marda.

Unfazed, Blue reached toward the sheath on her belt loop and folded her fingers around the handle of an identical knife. "I learned my lesson last time, Marda. These days, I'm always prepared for life's little emergencies."

"I'll kill her," Marda snarled. "Get away from the door. Move it."

Before Blue could answer, the guy yelled, "Let her go!"

"Dougie," the blond girl called out. "Stay back. She's crazy."

"Let her go!" The guy drew his fist back and slammed it into the side of stand-in Marda's head.

Marda shrieked and dropped the knife.

The blond girl rolled aside.

Blue leapt, and moments later, she straddled the Marda stand-in's body and pressed the edge of the blade against her neck.

"No!"

"Well, well, well, isn't this a familiar standoff?"

Stand-in Marda strained, but Blue pressed her advantage with the knife.

"Blue!" Rebecca's voice reached her, full of urgency. "That's not Marda, Blue. Remember that. That's not really Marda. It's just a shell, a body Marda took over, just a few minutes ago."

The Marda stand-in strained and pressed against the knife. "I'm quite willing to slay this body to make you move."

Blue threw her knife aside but reached out and pinned the body down with both hands. "Rebecca, if you have a thing you can do, now's the time."

"On it." Rebecca crouched next to the woman and placed a hand on either side of the woman's head. "Leave this body!" She commanded. "Return to the spirit realm. Leave this body and never return to another. I forbid it."

"You forbid?" The woman still struggled. "You cannot forbid me. You don't have that power."

Beneath Blue's hands, the body gave a final shudder, then went slack.

Rebecca stared intently at the inert form. "Actually, I do."

A moment later, the woman's eyelids fluttered and she opened her eyes. Her confused look could not be faked. "Who are you? What's going on? Get off me."

Blue rolled off the girl.

The woman struggled into a sitting position. "We were in the circle...about to contact the ghost..."

"Okay, seriously, get the hell out of my house," Blue snapped. "Now."

Rebecca flashed her badge at the guy.

His eyes squinted, then widened. "Agent?"

Rebecca made a show of producing her cell phone. "I'm calling the police. You three should not be here when they arrive."

"What happened?" The Marda stand-in asked.

The guy and the blond girl were already on their feet. The boy reached toward the Marda stand-in. "Later. Let's just go."

The three were out the door before Rebecca finished dialing.

Blue sighed. *Great. Another long night answering questions at the police station.*

"Hello? Is this Paul, or is this Jim?"

Blue and Chip exchanged a look. *So she's not calling the police after all.*

"Paul, I'd like for you and Jim to please bring the bottle of wine and enough glasses for everyone to share. Also, bring food appropriate for a celebration. Do you know where Leona's home is? ...Great. We'll see you soon."

Rebecca ended the call and pocketed her phone. She then dropped to the ground in front of the candle, which still burned bright in the middle of the rug. She motioned for Blue and Chip to join her on either side. "Where those three failed, I suspect we'll have better luck."

Blue looked at Chip. She read the look he returned as: *Why not?*

The three of them surrounded the candle and clasped hands. A palpable energy surged between them that gave Blue a bizarre buzz.

"Leona Shaefer," Rebecca spoke. "Leona, your daughter is here. On this night of restless spirits, please find your way to her. I will serve as your beacon."

Rebecca turned to Blue, her eyes burrowing in their intensity. "Blue, say something."

"Uh...Mom...It's Christmas Eve. Please come out. I want to wish you Merry Christmas." After a short pause, "I love you."

Still sitting in her chair, Sylvia spoke instead. "Don't you worry none, she's comin'."

Rebecca answered, "Thank you, Sylvia."

Blue stifled a chuckle. *Figures Rebecca and Sylvia are on a first-name basis.*

And then her mother was there, and Blue forgot everything else.

A figure... a vision of a dignified business woman with graying hair and the hint of crow's feet in the corners of her eyes... sat in the corner of the covered couch. Exactly as Blue had seen her many times in life, and in a handful of visions and dreams.

The specter's eyes reflected somber sadness.

"Mom!" Blue's voice broke. The emotion of the moment overwhelmed her, to see her mother, so lifelike, in the room with them.

The specter looked over at the three figures, and the barest trace of a smile showed on her sad features.

"Mom..., it's... it's Christmas Eve," Blue said. It sounded lame in her ears. "It's... good to see you, Mom."

The specter spoke, its voice cracking. "Fiona. Please... tell me you are doing well. I miss you so much."

"I miss you, too. It's so—" Her voice caught.

Chip's hand squeezed hers, and she realized something. "Mom... this is Chip. Eugene Farren. The guy I told you about the night that.... Well, we're... together."

"We met," Chip offered, "sort of, in a dream. Hello, Ms. Shaefer. It's good to see you..." he hesitated.

Blue realized his quandary. *What do you say to a ghost? 'In person?' 'In the flesh?'*

"While awake," he finished.

The ghost cracked a smile. "Thank you, Chip. Thank you for protecting my little girl."

Blue wrested her gaze from her mother to look at Rebecca. "If I tried, could I... can I hold her?"

To Blue's surprise, Rebecca nodded. "The paranormal forces are strong now, you should take advantage of—"

But Blue was already on her feet, and mother and daughter locked in a tender hug.

Blue sat next to her mother on the couch. Her tears wet a spot on her mother's shirt. Her mind raced with questions about how that worked, but she ignored them. "This is...the best Christmas present I could possibly ask for."

Delicate fingers stroked Blue's hair. "Me, too, baby. Me, too."

The door creaked open behind her, and Blue pulled herself into a seated position.

Her dad walked in first, followed by Jim. Her dad's eyes widened at the sight of his estranged, dead lover and the mother of his only child sitting and looking at him from across the room.

"I...my God, Lee..." Words failed him, and the bottle of wine and containers in his hand began to slip.

Chip rushed forward, caught the items, and backed away.

Leona, too, looked away. "Paul, I—"

Blue reached out and put a hand on her mother's lap, then reached with her other hand toward her father.

"Please... Dad. Don't ask how. She's here, for a little while. It's... what Rebecca does."

Paul held a clenched fist before his mouth as his eyes widened. Blue could see him try to accept this impossible moment.

Finally, his body shuddered and he dropped his hand. "Lee... it's... it's good to see you. Truly."

Her mother didn't smile, but answered, "Thank you, Paul. I'm... sorry."

"No," Her dad's voice cracked. "Don't waste time on that. It's fine." After an awkward pause, he started again. "I'm taking good care of her, Lee. As soon as I heard, I took her in. Fiona is growing into a very special person. I'm very proud of her. She's safe and she's happy."

Her mom said nothing, but her eyes glistened.

Her dad looked away from the ghost and looked at Blue as if for guidance, "What's appropriate here? Is Merry Christmas even the right thing to say?"

Unable to see from her own tears, Blue reached out toward each of her parents. "Just come here, both of you."

Blue basked in the midst of a warm, loving embrace, her sniffles mingling with the rest. With every moment, she was afraid her Mom would vanish without warning.

The three of them separated some time later, and Blue faced Chip.

He held out a wine glass half-filled with red liquid.

She accepted it gratefully.

Rebecca extended her own filled glass. "Blue, I'm glad I could do this for you, brief as it must be. In a fair universe, your mother

would be here with you, in the flesh, enjoying the holidays. Unfortunately, I can't make that happen. Nevertheless, Merry Christmas."

Blue sat, speechless. The wine tasted sweet, then bitter; the hint of chocolate and raspberry made for a decadent aftertaste.

She couldn't talk, and if she could, she wouldn't have been able to express her gratitude. Rebecca Burton creeped her out, but she also had saved her sanity, her future, and now had made this moment possible.

She found her voice. "Dad?"

"Yes, hon."

"Would it be possible to...that is... well... can I buy the house?"

Paul's shocked expression faded as fast as it had appeared. "You inherited the house. It's yours. We just have to take it off the market. The estate has been making payments for...." He stopped in mid-recitation. "But, do you realize what you're saying?"

Chip turned to face her. "You said... you never wanted to return to Perionne, ever again."

"I know what I said, but... Look, I still have years of school. It's not like I'm moving in tomorrow." She turned toward the vision of her mother. "But a girl's entitled to change her mind."

"Indeed she is," said Rebecca. "And on a related topic, a few weeks ago, I had offered you a job."

"On Team Rebecca. I remember. But then you rescinded the offer after I—"

"After I said I needed time to think about it. I have done so."

Blue noticed the curious look her father gave them both, but followed Rebecca's lead and pretended she didn't see it.

Rebecca continued, "If you're still interested, I will pay you a visit after the semester restarts so we can discuss details."

Once again stunned speechless, Blue could only nod.

Rebecca raised her glass. "To Christmas. A time for remembering. A time for new beginnings. May tonight be a joyous new beginning for all of us."

# About the Author

*"Blue Christmas" ties into R.J. Sullivan's paranormal thriller series published through Seventh Star Press. The series features headstrong punk girl "Blue" Shaefer, her nerdy boyfriend "Chip," and the mysterious paranormal investigator Rebecca Burton. R.J's short fiction has appeared in the acclaimed anthologies* Vampires Don't Sparkle *and* Dark Faith: Invocations. *Learn more at http://www.rjsullivanfiction.com*

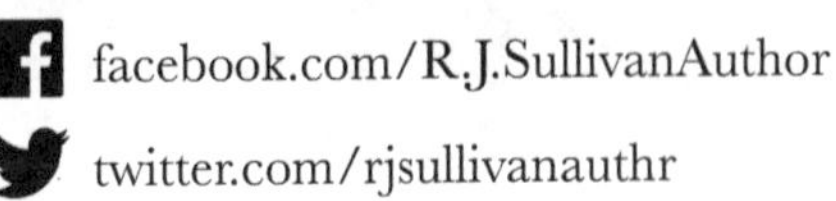
facebook.com/R.J.SullivanAuthor
twitter.com/rjsullivanauthr

## Also Available from R.J. Sullivan!
## Ghosts, Demons, and more Rebecca Burton!

Softcover ISBN: 978-1-941706-05-3
eBook ISBN: 978-1-941706-06-0

Softcover
ISBN: 978-1-93792987-9
eBook
ISBN: 978-1-937929-88-6

Softcover
ISBN: 978-1-937929-32-9
eBook
ISBN: 978-1-937929-33-6